WHERE IS M, ,,,,,,,:

WRITTEN BY: SHELINA KERMALLI
ILLUSTRATED BY: SAKEENA PANJU

"During my period of ghayba, you will benefit from me just as you benefit from the sun when it goes behind the clouds and is veiled from your sight. I am the source of refuge and protection for the people of the Earth."

IMAM MAHDI (AS)
KAMAL AD-DIN WA TAMAM AN-NI'MAH

IN THE NAME OF ALLAH, THE KIND, THE MOST MERCIFUL

Published by Sun Behind The Cloud Publications Ltd
PO Box 15889, Birmingham, B16 6NZ
First edition published in 2010
by Hasanaat in the United States of America
Text Copyright Shelina Kermalli © 2017
Illustrations Copyright: Sakeena Panju © 2017
ISBN: 978-1-908110-42-8

A CIP catalogue record of this book is available from
The British Library

www.sunbehindthecloud.com

Shelina Kermalli dedicated her life to children's education; from her degree in Elementary Education, to her volunteering in the local Madaaris and several other non-profit agencies, to homeschooling her own 3 children, Kamilah, Hasan, and Zahra.

Although Shelina's lifetime was short, her impact was profound. She left this world in 2016 at the age of 32 during the blessed month of Ramadhan and the nights of Qadr, and is fondly remembered by family, community, and friends alike as a "pure soul" who lived her life with grace and beauty, and was always ready to assist others. One of her oft-remembered pieces of advice to her own children was to always begin the day with a "salaam" to our living Imam (as) in order to build that connection with him and prepare for his return.

We pray that Allah (swt) showers His blessings upon Shelina, and covers her with His mercy, peace, generosity, and kindness.

Please recite a Surah Fatiha for the benefit of Shelina Kermalli.

NOTE TO READERS

In the name of Allah, the most Beneficent, the most Merciful.

"Allah has promised to those of you who believe and do good that He will most certainly make them rulers in the earth as He made rulers those before them, and that He will most certainly establish for them their religion which He has chosen for them, and that He will most certainly, after their fear, give them security in exchange; they shall serve Me, not associating anything with Me; and whoever is ungrateful after this, these it is who are the transgressors."

Holy Qur'an, Surah Noor, 24: 55

Allah (swt) sent Prophets and Imams as guides and warners. The death of the last Prophet Muhammad (saw) marked the end of Prophethood and the beginning of Imamat. Allah (swt) appointed twelve infallible Imams, or leaders, with the final one being Imam Mahdi (as). Imam Mahdi (as) is alive right now, and even though Allah has kept his identity hidden, we have certain responsibilities towards him during this time of ghayba.

Through this story I hope that children will come closer to and form a bond with the twelfth Imam.

The characters in this story are fictional, but the information about Imam Mahdi (as) is true.

"One who dies while he does not know the Imam of his time, dies the death of Jahiliyyah (the period of Ignorance before the time of the Prophet)"

Imam Ja'far As-Sadiq (as), Biharul Anwar

May our knowledge and love for Imam Mahdi (as) blossom and may we be among his helpers, followers, and defenders when he reappears-Ameen.

Please note the following Arabic terms are used in this book out of respect for God and the Prophets and Imams:

saw (ṣall Allāhū 'alayhi wa ālihi wa sallam):
Peace be upon him and his family
swt (subḥānahu wa ta'ālā):
Glory be to Him (God) the Most High
as ('alayhi al-salām):
Peace be upon him

Shelina Kermalli 2010

One sunny Sunday afternoon, Maysum and Sumayya arrive home from their weekend Islamic school.

"Assalamu alaykum children. How was Madressa today?" Mom asks.

"Wa alaykum as-salaam Mommy," both children answer.

"Sister Khadija taught us about the 12th Imam. His name is Imam Mahdi (as)," Sumayya says.

"That's wonderful! Did you know that Imam Mahdi (as) is the Imam of our time?" asks Mom.

"You mean he's alive right now?" asks Maysum.

"That's right!" Mom says, "Now come and eat your lunch before it gets cold."

Later that day, Maysum and Sumayya go outside to play hide and seek.

"Common Maysum, where are you?" asks Sumayya. She looks up towards the sky and notices the soft and fluffy clouds gracefully floating in front of the sun. The sun is playing hide and seek too, thinks Sumayya.

"Boo!" yells a familiar voice. Sumayya spins around and finds that her brother has found her instead.

"Where were you?" asks Sumayya.

"In the best hiding spot ever!" declares Maysum with a huge grin on his face as he points towards the slide.

At the end of the game Sumayya asks, "Maysum, where is our Imam? We have to know where he is so that we can follow him."

Maysum looks around the backyard and thinks about his younger sister's question. "Hmmm, that's a good question. I don't know where he is. Let's go and find him!"

Both of them start walking together in search of the 12th Imam.

They look behind trees and under park benches.

"Look, there's Ahmed and Anisa, let's ask them if they know where our Imam is!" suggests Maysum.

"Assalamu alaykum Maysum and Sumayya," Ahmed says, "Where are you going?"

"Wa alaykum as-salaam," they answer.

"We're trying to find the Imam of our time, but we can't find him anywhere," says Maysum.

Ahmed and Anisa also do not know where the Imam is, so they join Maysum and Sumayya in the search.

As the children continue looking for Imam Mahdi (as), they pass more trees, houses, and shops, but they still cannot find their Imam; however, they do notice two more friends- Ammar and Ameera.

After greeting each other Sumayya asks, "Do you know where the 12th Imam is? We want to find him so that he can guide us on the right path."

Ameera pauses for a moment and taps her chin thoughtfully, "We have never looked for him before, but he must be around here somewhere helping people out."

The large group of children continue to search for their Imam. Along the way they come across the mosque.

"Why don't we look for the 12th Imam in the mosque? The mosque is like the house of Allah and he is an Imam of Allah so he might be there," suggests Maysum.

The children enter the mosque just as the teachers from the Madressa are leaving. Sumayya sees her teacher, Sister Khadija, leaving and calls her name, "Sister Khadija! Assalamu alaykum, we need your help!"

"Wa alaykum as-salaam," Sister Khadija answers, "What are all of you children doing here long after the Madressa has finished?"

"During class you said that Imam Mahdi (as) is our Imam-our leader. We're trying to look for him so that we can follow him," explains Maysum, "but we can't find him anywhere."

"Oooh!" says Sister Khadija, seeing where all the confusion is coming from. "Let me explain. Imam Mahdi (as) is our leader, but he is in ghayba right now. He is living in this world, but Allah has made it so that we are not able to recognize him. Imam Mahdi (as) was only five years old when he became the Imam of our time. His life was in danger.

Allah (swt) has kept the identity of the Imam hidden to protect him from any enemies and to make sure that he is always here to guide us.

When Allah (swt) decides that the time is right, then our Imam will reappear and bring peace all over the world. But, even now, Allah lets the Imam visit people in need if they call on him," explains Sister Khadijah.

Sumayya smiles, "that's just like when we were playing hide and seek before, Maysum. You hid under the slide and I couldn't find you for a while. Even though I didn't see you, you were still there and could see me."

"That's right! Then I jumped out and surprised you!" remembers Maysum.

"But why does the Imam have to stay in ghayba for such a long time?" wonders Ammar.

Sister Khadijah explains, "Allah will send the 12th Imam when there are enough faithful Muslims to help him. In the meantime, we must get to know our Imam better and increase our love for him.

"What should we do while we're waiting for Imam Mahdi (as)?" questions Maysum.

"We should offer our salaams to him everyday, give sadaqa for his safety, volunteer in the community and help people in need, and learn more about Islam and stay away from bad actions," replies Sister Khadijah.

"How will we know when Imam Mahdi (as) reappears?" asks Ahmed.

"Allah will make his arrival known to the whole world. At that time, there will be a heavenly voice announcing that the Imam has reappeared, and if we are among the best of believers, then when we answer the call, we will all of a sudden be taken to Makkah to be with the Imam," describes Sister Khadijah.

"Wow!" exclaim the children.

"So we don't need to look for him anywhere- Allah will send him when the time is right. Thank you for explaining that to us Sister Khadijah," says Sumayya.

"Can you tell us more stories about the 12th Imam?" asks Anisa.

"Sure...next week at Madressa," answers Sister Khadija, "but for now, let us recite the du'a for the protection and safety of Imam Mahdi (as).

بِسْمِ اللهِ الرَّحْمَنِ الرَّحِيمِ

Bi-smillāh al-Raḥmān al-Raḥīm

In the name of Allah, The Beneficent, The Merciful

اللّـهُمَّ صَلِّ عَلَى مُحَمَّد وَآلِ مُحَمَّد

Allāhumma ṣallī ‘alā Muḥammad wa āli Muḥammad

O Allah, bless Muhammad and the family of Muhammad.

اَللّهُمَّ كُنْ لِوَلِيِّكَ الْحُجَّةِ بنِ الْحَسَنِ

Allāhumma kun li-walīyika al-Ḥujjat ibn al-Ḥasan

O Allah, be, for Your representative, the Hujjat (proof), son of Al-Hasan,

صَلَواتُكَ عَلَيْهِ وَعَلى آبائِهِ

Ṣalawātuka ‘alayhi wa ‘alā ābā’ih

Your blessings be on him and his forefathers,

فِي هذِهِ السّاعَةِ وَفِي كُلِّ ساعَةٍ

Fī hādhihī al-sā‘at wa fī kullī al-sā‘at

in this hour and in every hour,

وَلِيّاً وَحافِظاً وَقائِداً وَناصِراً وَدَلِيلاً وَعَيْناً

Walīyan wa ḥāfiẓan wa qā’idan Wa nāṣiran wa dalīlan wa ‘aynan

a guardian, a protector, a leader, a helper, a proof, and an eye,

حَتّى تُسْكِنَهُ أَرْضَكَ طَوْعاً وَتُمَتِّعَهُ فِيها طَوِيلاً.

Ḥattā tuskinahu arḍaka ṭaw‘an Wa tumatti‘ahu fīhā ṭawīlan

until You make him live on the earth, in obedience (to You), and cause him to live in it for a long time.